by Stan and Jan Berenstain

HarperCollins *Children's Books*

Trademark of Random House Inc., Authorised User HarperCollins Publishers Ltd.

CONDITIONS OF SALE

This edition published in the UK by HarperCollins Children's Books in 2009

1 3 5 7 9 10 8 6 4 2

ISBN 13: 978-0-00-730581-0

Visit our website: www.harpercollins.co.uk

Printed and bound in Hong Kong

One bear.

One wheel.

One bear on one wheel.

Two bears on one wheel.

Three on one.

Four on one.

Four bears on one wheel.

One bear on two wheels.

Four on two.

One on one again.

One on one.

Three on three.

None on four.

Four on none.

One on one again.

Five on one.

Five bears on one.

Five bears on none.

Ten on one.

One bear on five wheels.

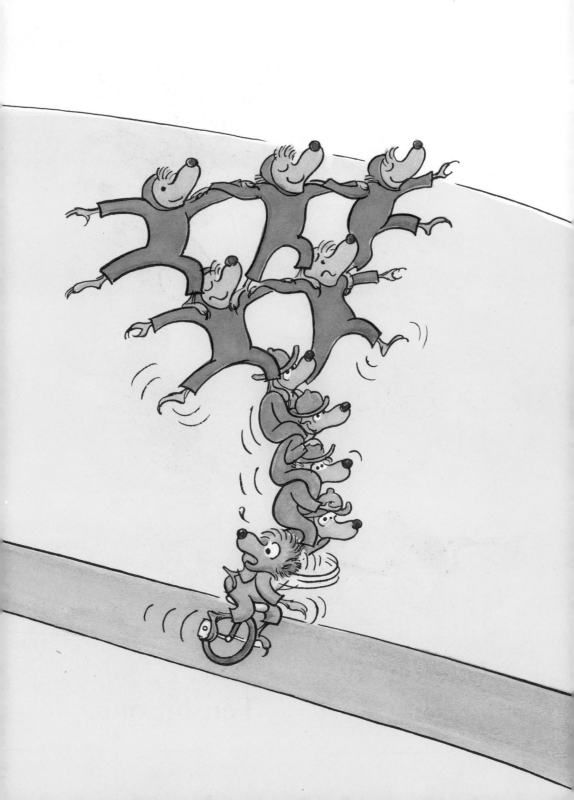

One on five.

Ten on one.

Ten on ten.

Twenty-one on none.

One on one again.